TRUTH, THUS HAPPINESS

A STORY BY
TOM J. GEORGE

© 2021 Tom J. George

Published by the author, and available through Amazon.com

ISBN: 978-1-7338972-5-9

Production services:
Populore Publishing Company
Morgantown, West Virginia

In memory of
Aunt Sarah H. George
who exuded truthfulness.

*Truth is the pedestal on which all
other virtues stand.*

— DR. P. RUU TUU

I

Weary of all the corruption in the news, I asked myself, *Why so much?* Weary of the growing dishonesty of our leaders, I worried, *Societal conduct is deteriorating, what is the reason for the growing decadence?* Tiring of the expanding profanity in my favorite pastime, evening Netflix movies, I wondered, *What's happening?* Curiosity prompted some research. Investigating, I tried to imagine our beginning as a society. What was our nation's founding value system? This line of questioning led me to the monumental gift of our Founding Fathers—the announcement of our independence.

The Declaration of Independence trumpeted our separation from the British Crown. It documented the fundamental principles for our governance. I have always appreciated the Declaration, but at the moment it felt awe-inspiring. I was trying to understand my deepening reverence for the founders' bold proclamation of our freedom. *Was it because I've aged, matured . . . the collection of life experiences since my youth?* Years back, I had casually checked off the Declaration of Independence and Constitution from an instructor's required reading list. Now, my regard for our founders seemed to be erupting into the highest level of esteem. *How could imperfect men create such a perfect founding document?* I couldn't recall anyone criticizing it. Our Constitution had its Bill of Rights and later amendments. But, the Declaration itself, "Perfect!"

We have a national holiday, and treasured symbols, that celebrate the system of governance our founders set in motion, and the principles that shaped a nation and created the unique people we have become. We display our flag in honor of the concept and honor it by solemnly promising:

> I pledge allegiance to the Flag of the United States of America, and to the Republic for which it stands, one Nation under God, indivisible, with liberty and justice for all.

At least, we made this commitment every morning of childhood public-school attendance. Now I wonder, *Why weren't we taught to do the same at home on weekends and school vacation days? Should more have been done to get us to see the significance of this pledge?* It's hard for me to understand and accept how, in recent times, the word *God* has become controversial. Today, a student may be excused from reciting the Pledge because of that word. Regardless, does recitation of the Pledge inspire improvement of social conduct? Would it be more palatable for that small group of discontents if instead of *God* we used *Creator?* But then, the Pledge would require yet another word, *our,* in order to read *under our Creator.* I decided that I would research the discussions held in contemplating the not-so-long-ago change to officially add *under God.*

First, I resorted to my favorite lookup site, Wikipedia, to gain a better understanding of the Pledge's meaning and purpose. I didn't remember being taught the Pledge's history. I didn't recall being taught that the first Pledge, not much like the present one at all, wasn't drafted until 1855 by George T. Balch, a Civil War veteran. The Pledge that evolved into today's version wasn't written until 1892, by Francis Bellamy, a Christian socialist minister. I was reminded that the now somewhat controversial words *under God* were added by Congress in 1954.

We express patriotism by singing the "The Star-Spangled Banner." But does the National Anthem promote constructive societal behavior over time? In the moment, it's inspiring to hear, but does the inspiration remain after "home of the brave?" As for special days, we have ten federal holidays. Only one, Independence Day, honors our proclamation of independence. On that day, the Fourth of July, we celebrate with fireworks and festivities. On the day before, the stock market trading stops three hours early, and other small gestures remind us that the day is significant. But, does the observance of the Fourth have any effect on the way we think and act? *I'm guessing maybe not a whole lot.*

To propel our children through the perilous, insecure moments of their future, what values must we instill in them now to inspire them to prevail against life's adversity and temptations? I fear these are not spelled out for us. Family, educational institutions, religion, and the justice system influence our conduct, but in a disjointed, piecemeal way. Does anything address the need for continual conduct improvement? If so, what, and how? Is the prescription for good, everyday conduct complex or simple? I've thought a lot about these questions searching for understanding.

Those of us who truly strive to be better citizens and better people need to use our minds to piece together the answers. And, not everyone wants to put in the effort. *Talk about an understatement.* It would be all good and well if the answers were clear, crystal clear, for our sake— and more importantly, for our children and theirs. Short of resorting to our respective religions or personal creeds for the values to instill into our children to preserve our founders' dream, how is it best done? What one-word values must we promote? Of the plethora of values, which one or which few are the highest priority?

II

I spend too much time thinking about all sorts of things. Lately, I've spent too much time thinking about "values." Quality time. I can get so absorbed in hypotheticals . . . pondering and reflecting on plans, concepts, objectives, especially about something I care about. In midlife, in a workplace seminar, the instructor administered a personality test. Later, he took me aside and whispered, "Tom, you have a creative personality. This is rare." I was thankful for learning a bit about why I was different from most—why I was always coming up with seemingly *bizarre* stuff and often saw solutions before many others. Yes, it was invigorating, but I had an ongoing and related challenge. My problem was learning how to excite others to help implement these solutions, to put the ideas to constructive purpose. A snag with solutions is they most often represent a need for change. Yet, change is often resisted; the greater the change, the greater the resistance. It was years before I learned to anticipate and manage such resistance.

Once retired, I continued to puzzle over how to frame real workplace problems, particularly interpersonal issues, in a way to inspire *collective* improvement. My professional success wasn't so much based on technical smartness. Rather, it was my always striving to draw other people into collective efforts for improvement. Upon leaving my engineering position in the Federal Government, I knew that I wanted to continue contributing. I decided that I would make my points for social improvement through writing. I would use scientific and engineering scenes to portray people problems, and how to overcome them. My plan seemed reasonable: I liked to write and had earlier committed to writing as a hobby in retirement. I would use fiction because I didn't have the needed education, reputation, or experience to be authoritative in speaking about and dealing with societal issues. I certainly didn't have the university degrees to write formal journal articles in the social and psychological sciences. But I *could* write fiction. It would be the means for me to try to help improve societal value systems.

Before retiring, looking ahead to a time with no job to go to, I had attended writing workshops at my local university. *I wasn't going to wait to the last minute—I liked to be prepared.* The workshops were a big help in my becoming a stronger writer. Also, I learned that I wasn't alone in the desire to write well and in the challenge of writing well. I had thought that writing fiction would be only fun. Instead, I discovered that writing good fiction was harder than practicing engineering. Though it may not be the most joyful experience, writing brought me— and continues to brings me—considerable satisfaction in my retirement years.

III

My first novel was set in a federal agency workplace. The project was gratifying but also demanding—especially the end. *Actually, it was all quite startling! Who knew where this pastime would take me?* About that ending: I was working on the last couple of pages and was stuck. One character was really struggling. He had imagined citizenship in a country of societal perfection—the United States. Instead, he discovered that no such heaven exists in America. My Korean leading man, "Proto," was causing me fits. I was trying hard to determine how he was going to end the book. Proto had his own mind and didn't like the ending I had in mind. What does a writer do? Ultimately, I let him have free rein. Soon he was acting more outrageous than in any of the previous pages of the novel. For the citizenship process, he had studied our country's history and government process. *Oh, he can sometimes be so private. He probably aced the naturalization tests, but never said a thing about it.* So, what does he do? My protagonist, inspired by his workplace experiences, flags a word in our Declaration of Independence's Preamble that he felt was wrong, one that needed replacing.

Imagine, he was granted US citizenship, and then a few years later he had the nerve to criticize a most sacred document. *Shocking! How dare a US citizen consider meddling with such revered words?* Well, no one would be so bold—until Proto. It shook me to witness the audacious Proto take issue with our Declaration. He did so out of a sense that the choice of a single word by our Founding Fathers was incorrect. Proto had in mind a word necessary for proper behavior of our leaders, in both the government and private sector. His idea seemed an enviable improvement. It was difficult to allow Proto to get away with his brazen lunacy. But, I was eager to end and publish the novel, and of the various endings I had considered, I liked this one best. *Plus, before I was deep into the novel, I recall reflecting on our Declaration of Independence, even going so far as to call it "Perfect!"* Hmm, interesting. I found myself allowing this character of my imagination to slam our precious Preamble. Incidentally, such outspoken honesty was an attribute that, though noble, wasn't conducive to Proto's professional success. Such temperament got him into trouble with managers seeking *yes-men* as subordinates. Try as they might, Proto's peers couldn't teach him to keep his mouth shut, or to convince him that even whistleblower laws wouldn't protect him. Now, the tables were turned. Proto, the character I invented, was putting words in *my* mouth.

As a matter of fact, I was increasingly receptive to this turn of events. *This, though, isn't what I thought I would be faced with as an author!* After retiring, several years had slipped by. The quickly passing time reinforced my worry of the growing unethical conduct of so many of our leaders. It seemed the societal value system of my youth had run amuck, and my anxiety was coming to the surface. In the imaginary world of my novel, Proto knew only confrontation. Despite the consequences, he was committed to rectify the slippage of workplace values. He ignored the reality that it meant trouble with his corrupt supervisors. In fear of retribution, most of us just watch in silence. Eventually, we succumb and let our own values slip to the level of the ones we at first saw as wrong. When this happens, we have undermined a pillar-stone of our precious country—liberty. We become prisoners of wrongdoing and relinquish our liberty for the sake of preserving our paychecks. We thus join the corruption and allow ourselves to be blind to the dishonesty surrounding us.

I worried I was becoming too preoccupied with Proto and his actions. I felt infected by that upstart's reasoning. In spite of that, I wanted to bring my book to a conclusion. So, I had one final debate with my own created character. I came around, thinking, *Wow! Proto, you are correct. Our Declaration of Independence could be improved significantly by changing one word. Your idea that* truth *is a better word than* happiness, *is right on —"life, liberty, and the pursuit of truth." This is powerfully better!* Proto had forced me to conclude my first novel, *Color of Delusion,* on his terms. But, at what cost?

I rationalized—none, because it was fiction. And now that Proto had become a real person in my mind, I couldn't let our lively conversation end, or let him simply disappear. I began working on a sequel.

IV

My desire to work on a sequel didn't last. I moved that idea to a back burner. But Proto's lunacy remained. His convictions stuck in my head. I had succumbed to my protagonist's cry for ethical improvement. *Improvement* was a word I knew well: In my professional career, I had been a lifelong practitioner of total quality management ("TQM," in the industry) principles. Though the focus of my working life was improvement to technical systems, I was crossing a border, stepping into the foreign country of behavior betterment. I agreed with Proto. Moral decay and corruption has always been around, but now it seems to be growing. *Proto, my friend, you have lit a fire under me. How did you do that?* I had to do something and settled on writing a story. *This story.* A story that would offer a solution, or at least bring attention to the *happiness/truth* problem. Maybe the story would be a request for help. *Maybe it would move more towards non-fiction than fiction?* We need suggestions for overcoming the dishonesty creeping into the fabric of US society. Blatant, shameful, unpunished lying of some leaders must stop. The challenge is how to plead for our ideas, how to create an environment to encourage more moral leadership.

Proto's proposal consumed me. He became more adamant, reminding me that corruption in leadership is a growing problem, "Tom, why not help our founders inspire our collective improvement? They risked all to establish the most unique system of governing ever." Proto's thinking had merit: the founding document of his adopted country implied honesty but didn't demand it—but it should! Proto persisted: "Tom, don't be a coward. Do something! Help fix your country's value system." But, being frank, I told myself not to be the one to announce that our value system was broken. I certainly didn't want to be portrayed like that. I didn't have the letters after my name or the hard data to prove the correctness of such a demand. *Yikes! Be the champion for such a cause?* It was too much. *The only response is to do nothing.* I searched for the rational thing to do, but I kept telling myself, *Tom, do nothing!*

I was torn. *Haunted, really.* Progressively obsessed. I was squandering time rationalizing Proto's absurdity. His seemingly irreverent provocation continuously taunted me. His dare was bold—too bold. He was daring me to search to show the illogic of his confrontational asser-tion. Now, I was resisting, feeling that he was impugning a venerated American tradition. If we Americans worship anything, it is the Declaration of Independence. Taking issue with the most revered sentence in our Declaration would invite rebuke, retribution. *Did I need that? Did I want to even mention it to others?* I feared that publicly promoting improvement in our Declaration of Indepen-dence would invite incredulous ridicule. *Should I help Proto? Do I promote, or even suggest for consideration, a change, a one-word edit, an altering of this document?* I shook my head. *Tom, how do you dare consider editing our Declaration! What are you thinking? Is this path cre-ative, bizarre, principled? What? What are you thinking?*

Proto's perhaps preposterous idea of an error in our national Declaration was now thoroughly embedded in the *give it very strong consideration area* of my perhaps too visionary mind. *Or, too open? Too gullible? Too vulnerable?* Fictional character though he was, Proto's idea was alluring to me. *No, it was compelling!* His spark of an idea was now lighting within me a bonfire of a "process improvement" opportunity. *One of my choice activities. Did I want to turn away from that? Especially one relating to something of great, urgent import. If nothing else, I can keep thinking about all of this for a while.* Proto had achieved citizenship believing in a purer US moral compass, a notion that was no longer our national reality. Finding the compass deficient, with unorthodox defiance he offered a fix. He felt his citizenship obliged him to act. He deplored standing around in silence. His demand was pushing me toward taking steps for the monumental— and momentous—edit he felt our country needed.

I was unable to banish Proto's dogged image. Over and over he chastised me to do something about the one-word slip-up. His lambasting was becoming a fever in my brain. The pain was unrelenting. His agony, now my torment, forced me to dig deeper, first in Wikipedia. I returned to the Preamble to the Declaration of Independence. I copied the document exactly, including the footnote indicating the physical location of the document's creation. Scrutinizing our Preamble, I dared imagine intervening on behalf of our Founding Founders. I cheered myself on, *The edits would benefit our children and theirs.* I pretended, *Mr. Jefferson, do you believe that the pursuit of* happiness *is really the best?* I imagined Mr. Jefferson's reaction, which disquieted me. It wasn't what he said, but the inquisitive look. Was I in a time warp of lunacy? At first weird, then puzzling, then mystifying, Proto's edit started feeling simply comfortable. Before, his edit felt right. Now it was feeling agreeably challenging rather than fearfully right. My feelings were shifting from annoyance for Proto's rightness to empathy. *Had I been brainwashed? Hook, line, and sinker?* I spoke aloud, "Proto, you have seduced me!" *Well, almost, perhaps.* I then repeatedly reread the Preamble, as is, for any improvement possibility. My initial reluctance was being overtaken by a compulsion for improvement, but with regret for allowing this man of my own invention to possess me.

V

From close scrutiny of our Preamble, I grew more respect for our Founding Fathers' talent and foresight. They expressed much in few words. With an open mind, not blind acceptance, I saw the need to study our Preamble. I hoped I wasn't feeling too cozy with Proto's gutsy mindset. I started realizing our founders not only gave us the right but an obligation to correct their mistake. Now, I was outright admitting that the Founding Fathers erred. My war of words with Proto lost, I read and reread:

Preamble to the Declaration of Independence

We hold these truths to be self-evident, that all men are created equal, that they are endowed by their Creator with certain unalienable Rights, that among these are Life, Liberty and the pursuit of Happiness.

Technically, a "preamble" comes at the beginning of a document, and this sentence is actually the beginning of the second paragraph of the Declaration. But it is so powerful, so revolutionary, that is has long been considered the *de facto* Preamble, strongly laying out the foundational idea of the entire document. Studying one of history's greatest prologues, I again worried, *Would I have any credibility? Is it sensible to think anyone would seriously consider the rantings of a fictional character?* On the last page of my novel, the protagonist wrestled to understand the purpose of America. He struggled with his understanding of the meaning of our primary national symbol: our red, white, and blue flag—our blessed Stars and Stripes. Proto saw that the key phrase "the pursuit of happiness" could be stated more powerfully. He asserted, "The founders chose the wrong word, *happiness*. A more esteemed value would have been better—*truth*, not *happiness*." My novel's protagonist surmised that some seek happiness by heinous means. The "pursuit of happiness" by Proto's workplace management chain focused on his destruction. In the most hostile, shameful manner, his superiors conspired for Proto's doom and, thus, were destroying his enviable scientific reputation. Their joy was the idea of ending the career of a scientist of international repute. Worse, it was for no reason other than jealousy.

My protagonist's sagacious reasoning was astonishing. How could this relatively new citizen, a Korean American, grasp a concept missed by so many long-time American citizens? A few folks may have discerned a view similar to Proto's. But, they didn't share it for fear of embarrassing feedback. The probability of public indignation would deter them. To Proto, social correctness was a foreign concept. The tactfulness of timely truthfulness eluded him. Do other authors have knotty Proto-like characters? This one enticed his author, me, to end a first book by allowing him to castigate our Founding Fathers. *Did I create a monster? What a character! My book was done, printed. Yet, he wouldn't leave me alone.* He tempted and tempted me to participate in his lunacy. Though I tried, I couldn't purge his observation from my psyche. Like a nightmare, his notion of this "mistake" possessed me. Proto's idea gyrated in my head, forcing me to wonder, *Should I assume Proto is right? Possibly* happiness *is not the best word the Founding Fathers could have used. Instead of* happiness, *what word is better? What good is the right to life and freedom if not to achieve a jubilant, joyful state of happiness?* With my mind captivated, as Proto's prisoner I was practically in his chain gang helping him try to improve the Federal Government. I had difficulty believing he almost had me slaving to replace the word *happiness* in one of our most celebrated government documents.

I reasoned that American citizenship is a state of being meant to bring those owning it immense happiness. Proto does make sense, I'll admit. He speaks from experience: Proto's story reminds us that the *selfish happiness* of a few of his managers was Proto's *unhappiness*. Likewise, a successful bank robbery might thrill the robber but cause unhappiness to many others. Pursuing happiness has boundaries, as when it is inconsistent with the right to life and liberty of others. My happiness must not be making others unhappy through purposeful, unsavory means. Playing a game and my winning might make the loser feel unhappy. But winning fairly and by the rules of the game is not unsavory. I should not pick a route to happiness that causes deliberate sorrow for others. But, the most important document doesn't say that. It says *pursuit* of happiness. It fails to explain that the pursuit should not be at the expense of others' happiness, at least not explicitly, which is a regret. How could the Declaration have been written, in the simplest way possible, to say this precisely? How can we declare that pursued happiness is only acceptable when achieved in legal, moral, respectful ways?

13

VI

Though I had to overcome some reluctance to do so, Proto's radical point of view was moving beyond simple acceptance. *Alas, I admit acceptance, after hours and hours, including sleepless nights, thinking about all of this.* Proto felt our founding documents should be written to ensure no mistake in our focus. In the ideal, our founding documents would frame with perfect clarity appropriate ways for achieving our "inalienable rights"—*life, liberty* and perhaps most important to most, *the pursuit of happiness.* Inspecting our nation's founding document should instill in us only noble, moral, magnanimous, honorable thinking. Our Declaration of Independence wasn't designed to promote happiness through hurtful means. No! Hurtful, harmful, or unhealthy means was not the intent of our Founding Fathers. Our founding document should be awe-inspiring. It should excite worthy striving toward noble values from birth to death. It's alright if we seek *unselfish* happiness. But, sometimes individuals focus on their happiness being the unhappiness of others. In our huge universe of words, is *happiness* the best word our founders could have chosen? We need a word conveying an unambiguous value. We need words that inspire us to higher levels of patriotic commitment to the cause our magnificent United States of America represents.

Maybe Proto's creator—me—had endowed him with too much persistence and persuasion. Proto had won his mind game with me. *I hoped he wouldn't insist that I sign a blood contract to make whatever sacrifice needed for a founding-document edit of a single word!* I got to work right away. I would search for the best replacement for the word *happiness.* How does one select a superior word to replace a lesser word in the document our Founding Fathers gifted us? Suppose such a word is found? How does one then justify it to others? And, who would those others need to be? I remember the words of my dear aunt Eva, lecturing me more than once, "You don't have to justify anything if you stay silent. Sometimes it's important to keep your mouth shut." So, I committed to a search. However, I promised myself I would use the results for only my personal satisfaction and not seriously propose or take any action.

My fictitional character's fixation was truthfulness. Blind pursuit of it caused Proto grief, incredible anguish. But, through all of the suffering, he took pride in doing the right thing—embracing his truthfulness. Though *truth* was an outstanding candidate for replacing *happiness* (as Proto had suggested), I thought it best to explore the implication of *truthfulness* rather than *truth*. In the courts, our justice system demands we testify truthfully. Many suspect the goal of prosecutors within our justice system is successful prosecution—the higher the number of convictions, the better. Many are coming to believe the goal should instead be to establish the truth in judicial matters. In normal life, speaking truth often requires discretion. Why? Truth can be used as a salve to heal, and truth can be used as a sword to harm. One would be hurt to learn a spouse is a cheating mate. Ill-timed announcement of the truth is upsetting. An error on a Federal tax form means one will incur financial penalty, and thus stress. Some situations cry for compassion to accompany truthfulness. Bad news of a relative's or friend's serious health issue should be shared with sympathy. It's wise to use tact to inform your supervisor that a concept for executing a project is flawed. For long-term supervisory respect, a boss should do the same when confronting a less-than-perfect subordinate. When revealing the truth may cause the recipient stress, decency suggests we manage how it is delivered, and the timing. Truthfulness should never be accompanied with insensitivity.

No doubt, *truth* and *truthfulness* deserved consideration as replacements for *happiness*, but I also wanted to evaluate other alternatives. I began a fairly exhaustive investigation for other best-candidate words to take the place of the value *happiness* in our Declaration of Independence. My search for articles on best or most preferred values started in the fall of 2020 at the WikiHow site, www.wiki.how.com. Entering the search term *"values,"* this interesting summary popped up one day:

1. How to define your personal values (318,529 views)
2. How to define your family values (176,426 views)
3. How to teach values (14,807 views)
4. How to inculcate human values (118,699 views)

Besides significant links for *values*, there were several Wiki advertisements promising lists of them. It seems there is a large market in the values business—professional development and the like. Maybe my caution to show interest in finding and in promoting the best values was unfounded. I wondered about speaking out personally, without making up a fictional character as a surrogate. I studied all pertinent Wiki articles and the values listed therein. Next, I searched the internet in general for articles on personal values. I entered search phrases such as *competing values, most important values, core values*, etc. Most postings listed only a few values, and thus revealed the author's favorites. Some articles rated the importance of competing values. I tried to note the most-repeated values but could find no consensus. One posting listed over 200 values. I hypothesized that there is an upper limit to the total number of words identifying values in our language, maybe between 220 and 250.

From my on-the-job TQM days, I recalled that many process improvement leaders claim work teams should choose their own 2–3 values to support an upcoming effort. That prompted me to name my three—*respect, faith*, and *love*—which I had found earlier in a religious setting. I found it easier to settle on a few rather than just one. I couldn't decide on a "favorite." For a quick minute, I looked at my three words and realized none would work in place of *happiness* in the Declaration. And, I recognized that of the dozens and dozens of other values I'd been seeing on my screen, none of them was resonating as "just the right word." During my evaluation process, however, Proto's fundamental principle kept coming to mind. It embodied a fanatical commitment to *truthfulness*. I used the heart of this word when I asked myself, "Tom, in *truth*, what is the best value to replace the word *happiness* in our Declaration?" *There's that word again*: truth. *Proto was preoccupied with its gravity and so am I. Pay attention, Tom!* Proto, whom I respected tremendously, was a man of truthfulness. He was an exemplary scientist, an international leader in materials research. Science is, *a quest for truth*. So, the more prominent a scientist, the more you might expect a truthful person.

"That's it! Yes!" I exclaimed loudly. If the word *happiness* needs replaced, it *must* be replaced with *truth*. I had made up my mind. I was sure. I would brave the consequences of folks observing my trying to improve our Preamble. *Oh, Tom. What was I doing? So much for the promise I'd made to myself! The one that I would use my research findings only for my personal satisfaction. Yup, I'm breaking that promise. I've come this far, I'm moving ahead.* I felt an urgency to see how it looked. Hear how it sounded. I typed, substituting the word *truth* for *happiness*. Then, looking at my screen, I read it aloud.

> We hold these truths to be self-evident, that all men are created equal, that they are endowed by their Creator with certain unalienable Rights, that among these are Life, Liberty and the pursuit of **Truth**.
>
> *(Edit 1 of Preamble)*

VII

Though generally an unemotional person, seeing this change in writing went beyond pleasing me. I was thrilled. Written out, the word *truth* felt much superior to the word *happiness*. Oh, how nice if we could actually swap the word *truth* for *happiness* in our Preamble. In a classic script font, 36 point, I printed the passage, which looked even better on paper. I hung the sheet just above my television and proudly reviewed my edit of our Preamble. I repeated this prideful habit during TV commercials. Daydreaming, I imagined someone with a beautiful speaking voice recording the passage and my rigging the TV sound system to mute during TV commercials, and play my recorded version of the Preamble. Even without such a silly setup, the passage made for a satisfying distraction, even sometimes during TV shows. I often found myself wondering, *Is scrutinizing a change to what has become a treasured word a worthwhile or a foolish exercise? Would I ever stop asking such questions?* Proto had convinced me of the rightness of his proclamation. He so convinced me, that my pride in having brought him into the world swelled. How can a sensible person be proud of a fictional character in a novel? *This wasn't like me. I was a no-nonsense kind of guy. Responsible and grounded. I hoped to avoid a psychiatric visit.*

My gratification lasted several days. It lasted until the day I noticed my editing was incomplete. Another edit was needed—one that at first seemed modest, straightforward, but which quickly moved to "not so fast, Tom." Our Preamble already contained the word *truths*. My deleting *happiness* and adding *truth* created a duplication—two *truths*: one plural, the other singular. As mistakes go, I tried to reason it was relatively insignificant. At first, I thought about trying to live with *truths* in the plural duplicated by *truth* in the singular. Though each implied differing meaning and purpose, my editorial oversight bothered me. Trying to improve our Preamble, Proto and I had created a bit of an ungainly sentence. *Ungainly? It was inelegant! How on earth did that get by me earlier?*

Over several days, I reviewed my lapse—the mistake, which now seemed so glaring. I must replace *truths* with the closest word of similar meaning. I thought maybe *fundamentals*. But, *fundamentals*, a good word, didn't cut it. It didn't have the power of the word *truths*. I searched and studied. I could find no overwhelmingly satisfactory replacement. *Must I insert a word that was okay but not great? Maybe.* At long last, I settled on *principles*, a synonym for *truths*. Though reluctant to make another edit, I caved. I decided both changes were necessary. Until someone suggests a better improvement of our most precious passage, it reads as follows:

> We hold these **principles** to be self-evident, that all men are created equal, that they are endowed by their Creator with certain unalienable Rights, that among these are Life, Liberty and the pursuit of **Truth**.
>
> (*Edit 2 of Preamble*)

I shared these two edits with friends, who warned that I should be cautious, "Tom, please don't become the character in your own book." They liked the character Proto in the book, but they preferred not having him as a personal friend. "We like you as you are." Some asked if this was a simple game or exercise to irritate. They implored, "Do you really want to risk publishing this proposal?" However, all admitted that the change would be an improvement. None suggested any additional edits. A few expressed fondness for the word *happiness*. None were patriotically bold enough to endorse my going public with a concept that might improve the fabric of American society. I'm sad to say, they all disappointed me. *None had ideas, even bits of ideas, for improving America's value system. Not one!* My friends encouraged me to pray, though, and I vowed to heed that suggestion as well as the one to be careful. I didn't tell them my prayer was for partners brave enough to team with me on the cause of promoting improvement of our value system. At this time, I also made a promise to myself: I would not take on my fictional character's persona. I must not enter Proto's never-never land of political incorrectness.

VIII

I tried to declare the Preamble editing exercise complete, but I couldn't. Something was missing. More weeks passed and then more. One night, deep in dreamland, an idea startled me awake. I sat up in bed, in the dark, and wondered, *Could we somehow get the word* happiness *back in?* I jumped from bed and, turning on lights along the way, I stumbled to my computer. Pulling up the Preamble file, I studied it, word by word. I had already failed my goal of introducing only a one-word edit. Now I was about to increase the edit count again, to three edits. *Oh, I'll just try it. Tom, don't worry, nobody will see it. You don't know until you try.* Mimicking Proto's over-the-top conduct, I found myself reinserting the word *happiness*. I placed it at the end of our Preamble, where it had originally appeared. However, even with this, the editing seemed incomplete. *This wasn't working at all. Time for something major! So much for simplicity and minimal edits.* I next inserted two words and even a punctuation mark: in front of the word *happiness*, I inserted *and, thus*.

> We hold these **principles** to be self-evident, that all men are created equal, that they are endowed by their Creator with certain unalienable rights, that among these are Life, Liberty, and the pursuit of **Truth, and thus, Happiness**.
>
> (*Edit 3 of Preamble*)

I set the three major edits in bold. I debated one word. *This is really getting to be a lot of changes. Are they all really necessary?* Would "Life, Liberty, and the pursuit of Truth, thus Happiness" be reasonable? After a time,

I decided that including the conjunction *and* was needed but wouldn't count as a significant edit. The change was in a positive direction but another change nonetheless. I summarized the main edits as follows:

Edit 1. Change: *happiness* to *truth*
Edit 2. Change: *truths* to *principles*
Edit 3. Add: *, and thus, happiness*

I was starting to hear the early-morning birds out back as dawn drew near. I now spoke aloud, as if Proto were with me, leaning against my kitchen counter, and asked, "How did I do?" *I think good! And, I even was able to use the word* thus. *I like that word.* I continued, "We keep key original concepts. We move the word *truth* to a place of more importance, greater impact. We keep *happiness*, but tie it to *truth*. What could be more important for our survival than ensuring we uphold the truth? What could bring about rethinking the best path, the ideal approach, other than that we should take to seeking happiness within the spirit I believe our Founding Founders wanted?"

As before, I printed my latest version, then set it on the table so I could review it while enjoying my first coffee of the day. Before pouring a second cup, I proclaimed my edits complete. I smiled for a few seconds, then straightaway identified a key question: Could the American Declaration of Independence—our nation's foundation—be changed? We can add amendments to the Constitution. But, we can't change the words that are already there. I assume our best legal and political scholars believe our Preamble is the introduction to our newborn nation's bold intention to make the people its highest priority. I assume most would claim it is so sacred it is neither editable nor amendable. But, I could find no such federal rule or law. *Truth be told, in my googling it was hard to know what words to even use in my searching.* Worse for me, hoping for some direction, I found no references of anyone suggesting such an outrageous idea of change. *Hmm. Too eccentric? Wacky me? Or, did I have something worthwhile here? Something worth sharing? Do I dare expose my odd thinking?*

IX

Time passed. But, my big question remained. I had an earth-shattering idea—should I risk putting it out there? *I know, easier said than done. You need specifics, Tom. Putting something out there is no easy task. Though it's just the first step, it has the potential for being a gigantic project.* I'm not afraid of hard work. What people think of me is not the issue. Being considered eccentric doesn't bother me. Not important. What I *do* care about is our embracing, living, and supporting the Preamble to the Declaration of Independence in the spirit that would make our Founding Fathers proud. My idea to improve the Preamble might be fantasy. To me, my fantasy is acceptable if it challenges each of us to strive for our improvement—individual and collective. My fantasy is acceptable even if it only inspires a single person to live a more patriotic life. And even if my idea were rejected, wouldn't it be great to have a serious national discussion of what the Declaration's Preamble means? If that could happen, I could handle some abuse along the way. Wasn't our individual and collective improvement the goal of our founders?

Okay, let's just say . . . if one were to identify sensible edits for a sentence or two in our Declaration of Independence, where would one begin? *I know, put it out there, but I want to think beyond that right now.* What might the conversation look like? How would it be done? Above all, I believe, unhurriedly. Why should it be slow? Why, perhaps, should we allow even decades for consideration of how best to improve our society and enhance the citizenship spirit within each of us? Indeed, a change such as this deserves profound deliberation, debate, dialog. Time would allow thoroughness in assessing the benefit, the cost, and the general acceptance. The benefits could be many, with our looking more closely at the values of *truth* and *happiness.* Our children, and theirs, would gain greater appreciation for our Preamble, even if it stays as written, just from taking the time to think deeply about it. Time is needed for anchoring and ingesting the founding purpose, original intent, and the hope our founders had for us and our children's children. *Hmm. If I take this on, I could be in for the long haul.*

X

A technical person, my working life embodied varied engineering activities. My work was easiest when there was a standard protocol for its execution. Most times, protocols existed. When there were no protocols, the practice was to pull a team of engineers together to discuss and decide the path forward. Twice, I approached international engineering societies for their standard to help me with work I was doing. In one case there wasn't a standard for an important point, and I was invited to sit on a committee the society formed to write one. In another situation, a standard existed, but it wasn't clear it applied for the dramatically new twist on technology of my then-current focus. I found myself on a committee updating the standard, and I soon had agreement that the standard as written was more than adequate for my situation. Now, with my Preamble project, I was in a nontechnical environment confronted with an outlandish social sciences issue—how to win support to edit our Declaration of Independence. I wondered if the social sciences professional community had developed any standards to guide our individual and collective behavior. And, how had they developed those standards?

Over several weeks, I wandered around the internet. I was getting a rudimentary introduction to the field and learning some of the professional jargon. I started with basic definitions to make sure I was roughly on the right track. I seemed to be. I found this in Wikipedia:

"Social science is the branch of science devoted to the study of societies and the relationships among individuals within those societies. The term was formerly used to refer to the field of sociology, the original 'science of society,' established in the 19th century."

I delved deeper and deeper, going from link to link. I saw seemingly endless popular-press and research articles—many of them highlighting data collection. I knew that gathering information would be critical if I were to champion my Preamble project. One article on Social Research caught my eye. The first sentence started, "The origin of the survey . . ." Surveys were something I knew about. Further down in the article it summarized the methodological challenges of the survey discussed in the article:

- Identify and select potential sample members.
- Contact sampled individuals and collect data from those who are hard to reach (or reluctant to respond).
- Evaluate and test questions.
- Select the mode for posing questions and collecting responses.
- Train and supervise interviewers (if they are involved).
- Check data files for accuracy and internal consistency.
- Adjust survey estimates to correct for identified errors.

All of this was a difficult read for an engineer. But, trying to understand led me to a conclusion: I must have the merits of my idea assessed through a survey. I realized that "*how* to propose and perhaps get an edit or edits made to the Declaration" needed to be low on my list for now. At the top must be determining if my idea could gain any traction with key people. Among the survey challenges would be (1) deciding what questions need addressed and (2) whom to ask. After weeks of trying to think this through, I decided two entities needed to be surveyed. It was imperative that I survey the US Congress. The intent of the survey would be not just to collect information but also to plant a seed for the concept of societal improvement. In thinking about this aspect of the purpose, it was obvious that the survey recipients must also include leading national journalists.

Identifying members of Congress (Senate and House) was straightforward. It was a bit harder to identify appropriate journalists to survey. The internet yielded a list of 200 top journalists. This implied surveying over seven hundred individuals (congressional members and journalists). *Goodness! With postage alone, this would cost a fortune.* The internal caution continued, *Is this going to be worth doing? Will I appear foolish? Will I appear a fool to family, friends? And the general public whose attention this activity might attract?* I suffered several weeks of self-doubt about the merits of the survey. I needed Congressional opinion on the merits of the idea of editing our Preamble. I needed the same from our nation's leading journalists. I worried, *Is this need going to be shared by anybody, a single soul?* With more internet searching I determined the size of the mailing. Congress has 535 voting members: 435 representatives and 100 senators. Again, turning to Wikipedia, I found a list of 413 political commentators. Before, I had been thinking only of print journalists, with that earlier list of 200. My more recent and in-depth searching reminded me that we also have many broadcast and social media journalists. Network TV, blogs, twitter, and the like. *Maybe I needed to understand the difference between commentators and journalists before committing to that list of 413 political commentators.*

I'd eventually get this into a spreadsheet, with all of the details, but quick figuring (535 + 413) suggested 948 surveys to be mailed. *Wow, ouch! The costs for this mailing would not be trivial.* Postage for an outgoing standard-sized business envelope is 55 cents. Enclosing a stamped return envelope would be another 55 cents. Just the cost of stamps was going to run over $1,000. Plus, there would be the cost of envelopes, stationery, and printing. I would draft the survey materials. But, was I going to address all of the envelopes, run around town to get copies, etc.? I probably would need help—more cost! Bottom line: it looked like my idea could cost a few thousand dollars. Was the Preamble idea to improve society worth the effort, worth the cost? For several weeks I debated the cost–benefit. Would the cost of executing this initiative for USA societal improvement instigate societal improvement? *I know, it could flop, with zilch benefit? Could it somehow do more good than harm? This societal improvement work was risky business. It wasn't for the weak, that's for sure. Such advocating would be a serious commitment. I wonder what the average return rate is for such surveys?*

XI

The daily witness of societal discontent and decay continued to irk me. I wasn't alone. In personal conversations, folks would agree on the erosion of our societal ethics and values. I continued observing our society sliding further down a slippery slope of societal decay. I worried that we as a society were becoming comfortable with the slippage of value systems, ethics. Increasingly, what used to be unacceptable was now acceptable—the "new norm." Others were expressing less discontent. With folks not volunteering concern, I would remind them that we must act to halt the loss of our societal values or face our collective demise. They would agree, echoing the common concerns. Nearly all stated the same frustration: little can be done—probably nothing. I would listen sympathetically and beg each one, "Please, what do you feel we could collectively do to reverse this deterioration of values? What more than pray and wait for God's answer?" I received no constructive answers. *Not one.* When I enjoyed conversation with clergy on the topic and asked specifically about the solution, the only answer was, "Pray." In summary, I heard no suggestions for collective action towards remediation.

I can be persistent. I noticed the puzzled looks on people's faces when I talked about suggestions for collective action towards remediation. Wondering if that phrase confused them, I would patiently give an example, proposing: Would you be interested in, let's say, a collective protesting of bad language in films finding its way to our children? For example, on the media's busiest night, we could organize a national picket against theaters showing films with excess nudity and foul language. Perhaps religious organizations could unite and announce a special boycott of the offending media. Out of respect for the conduct God expects of His peoples, His followers would cancel their online film subscriptions, and make it clear that their action was in response to immoral scenes, conduct, and language. I don't know if my example was helpful or not. *How could it not be? Isn't it obvious that for change people need to band together and take a stand? Make a statement? Take action? This is our future! Our nation's future.* All I found was silence—with lots of confused looks thrown in. Also, again, a few were saying "Pray, Tom, pray." I would be going out on this limb alone.

I still believed the best tool to bring my concern for value systems in decline to national attention was a survey directed at the two targeted groups—Congress and journalists. Honestly, I have a hard time imagining myself asking people to answer a survey, because I detest the annoyance of receiving them myself. As I see it, I have no choice but to give it a try. I will proceed basically as I'd decided weeks back: reach out to senators, representatives, and political commentators. I have high hopes these are people who might influence action—if they agree with me. I think, if I can convince just one nationally recognized individual to help, that would be a big win.

XII

I have participated in many surveys, but never initiated one. I must give it my best shot. *That's all I can do. I've come a long way! It's hard to believe I made it to a place to at least act on a national concern. I'm feeling good that I'm now at least committed to try.*

Many days passed since letting go of any and all concerns for personal embarrassment. I began to research how to conduct a formal survey. Until then, I hadn't given much thought to the alternatives—through the mail, on the telephone, in person, or by computer. Up to this point, I had been assuming I would do a survey through the mail. Nevertheless, I wanted to really study the options and give each one careful consideration. I convinced myself that through the mail was most appropriate. I set about designing a survey that would fit on a single, standard sheet of paper. At first, the task seemed simple. I completed a very rough draft in an hour or so. But over time, I edited it repeatedly to improve the clarity, to simplify. Now a transmittal letter was needed to accompany the survey. This ended up being more challenging than imagined. Best I can remember, I have never edited a document so many times. Finally, I had both a letter and a survey instrument that satisfied me.

Initially, my plan was to send this short story to Congress along with the survey and its cover letter. However, the proofing, laying out, and printing of my story is a little behind. It will not be ready by the time the new Congress is to be seated. So, instead of delaying my early 2021 mailing, I decided to go ahead with the survey and promise a copy of the story as a thank-you to survey respondents. To indicate credentials in my ability to self-publish, in the letter's postscript I include citations of three other published works that are on Amazon. In this way, people receiving the survey will know my seriousness. On the back of the letter, I might include a short biography.

In summary, my work ahead will include:

1. Survey Congress and leading national political commentators.
2. Within a few weeks of the survey's distribution, publish this background document.
3. Use the survey results to grow this short story into a full-length book.

Hopefully, this approach is sensible. Maybe this effort, in some humble way, will contribute to sustaining and improving the United States of America value system.

Proposed
Survey Letter

[full name, properly titled]
[address L1]
[address L2]
[address L3]

Dear Senator [last name],
[or] Dear Mr./Ms. [representative's name],
[or] Dear [journalist's name],

The value system of the United States of America frames the worthiness of our government and governance. We have an abundance of law. But, what key values underpin our USA society? The Preamble of the Declaration of Independence suggests inalienable rights (values) are *life, liberty* and the *pursuit of happiness.*

A fundamental right related to *truthfulness* is not explicitly stated. In a short story, I edited our Preamble to include truthfulness:

> We hold these **principles** to be self-evident, that all men are created equal, that they are endowed by their Creator with certain unalienable rights, that among these are Life, Liberty, and the pursuit of **Truth, and thus, Happiness.**

In comparing the above to our Preamble, *principles* replaces *truths. Truth* replaces *happiness*, but the preferred path to it is given an American distinction. The right to pursue *happiness* remains. Unlike in the current Preamble, pursuing *happiness* by nefarious means is disqualified.

Upon my receipt of your copy of the attached survey and/or response, I will send you a copy of the short story *Truth, Thus Happiness*. Survey results will be incorporated into an expanded work.

Respectfully,
Tom J. George

PS: The above will join my other books found on Amazon.com (*Color of Delusion, Religion's Greatest Need,* and *A Whistleblower's Lament*).

CC: President, Vice President, Congress, Journalists
Attachments: (2) – Survey Instrument, Commentary

Importance of Truthfulness

1. Do you believe our societal truthfulness needs significant improvement?   Yes   No

2. The idea of editing the Preamble of the Declaration of Independence to encourage the pursuit of truth is:
    a. Sensible
    b. Ridiculous

3. Considering alternative values such as the following: justice, freedom, respect, community, etc.:
    a. Is *truthfulness* the most important societal value?   Yes   No
    b. What value is more important?

4. Explicit promotion of *truthfulness* would result in a significant decrease of societal problems—discrimination, abuse of power, etc.?   Yes   No

General comments:

About the Author

In 1975, while working as an engineer on US government energy projects, Tom George wrote a story on pneumatic coal transport, and was awarded a Certificate of Excellence by the Society for Technical Communication, besting an international pool of over 900 technical writers.  The honor did not prompt him to forsake engineering for a career in literature, but maybe it did plant a seed, because now in "retirement" Tom is writing with some of the same vigor he brought to his profession.

Tom's early hands-on technical work was as an Engineering Duty Officer in the US Navy, supervising construction and testing of warships. Next, after an MS in engineering, came certification as a Registered Professional Engineer. In a career spanning forty years, Tom has developed training manuals, designed and inspected aerial tramways, worked on coal gasification and liquefaction, patented two processes for improving fuel cells, and done important work in engineering cost analysis, boiler test standards, cooperative research on turbine systems, and electricity grid design.

Tom has also devoted much energy to community service, advocating for neighborhood preservation and restoration and for sensible planning in his home city of Morgantown, West Virginia. Tom spends much of his leisure time in carpentry; online investing; hiking and backpacking; kayaking and sailing; thinking about faith, society, values, and democracy; and, of course, writing.

About **Color of Delusion**
(The novel inspiring *Truth, Thus Happiness*)

Dr. P. Ruu Tuu's grandfather and mentor—his *halabeoji* in Korean—never forgot the brave Americans who came across the ocean to defend him and his home during the Korean War, so the boy grew up in the knowledge that the United States was the land of honesty and virtue. And so it seemed as he emigrated to Virginia, undertook a career as a professor of engineering, married an American, and began raising two precious daughters.

As his family grew, so did his lab duties at Oak Forest University, and soon there was not enough time in the day to give both sides of his life the attention needed. When he was offered a supervisory office job at the National Materials Laboratory of the US Department of Defense, Proto—as he became known in America—was happy to accept.

Proto's belief in America as a haven of truth and virtue died at the gate of the NML. From the collegial structure of the university, where the deans at the top of the hierarchy understood and appreciated the areas they administered, he was plunged into the federal bureaucracy's system of career bureaucrats directing the work of professionals. The result was small-minded animosity, large-scale waste of time and materials, and workers discouraged or prevented from doing their work.

When the boot of bureaucratic corruption stepped on Proto's toes, his closest friend Sonia advised eating a little dirt, keeping a low profile, and going about his job. But the other guiding voice was that of his beloved *halabeoji*, who taught him that a just man must fight injustice wherever he finds it.

Tom George's novel *Color of Delusion* follows Proto on his determined battles on behalf of honesty.

Made in the USA
Monee, IL
21 February 2021